PUFFIN BOOKS

Take a Good Look

...ine Wilson writes for children of all ages. ...itcase Kid won the Children's Book Award, ...e Act won the Smarties Prize, and The ...trated Mum won the Guardian Children's Book ...e Year Award.

...queline lives near London in a small house ...med with 10,000 books.

Take a Good Look

Jacqueline Wilson

ILLUSTRATED BY
Stephen Player

PUFFIN BOOKS

For Jessica, with many thanks

PUFFIN BOOKS

Published by the Penguin Group
Penguin Books Ltd, 80 Strand, London WC2R 0RL, England
Penguin Putnam Inc., 375 Hudson Street, New York, New York 10014, USA
Penguin Books Australia Ltd, 250 Camberwell Road, Camberwell, Victoria 3124, Australia
Penguin Books Canada Ltd, 10 Alcorn Avenue, Toronto, Ontario, Canada M4V 3B2
Penguin Books India (P) Ltd, 11 Community Centre, Panchsheel Park, New Delhi – 110 017, India
Penguin Books (NZ) Ltd, Cnr Rosedale and Airborne Roads, Albany, Auckland, New Zealand
Penguin Books (South Africa) (Pty) Ltd, 24 Sturdee Avenue, Rosebank 2196, South Africa

Penguin Books Ltd, Registered Offices: 80 Strand, London WC2R 0RL, England

www.penguin.com
First published by Blackie and Son Ltd 1990
Published in Puffin Books 1993
Reissued in this edition 2001

020

Text copyright © Jacqueline Wilson, 1990
Illustrations copyright © Stephen Player 2001
All rights reserved

Set in 15/20 pt Postscript Monotype Baskerville
Typeset by Rowland Phototypesetting Ltd, Bury St Edmunds, Suffolk
Printed in England by Clays Ltd, St Ives plc

ISBN 0-141-30942-3
ISBN-13: 978-0-14-130942-2

www.greenpenguin.co.uk

MIX
Paper from
responsible sources
FSC™ C018179

Penguin Books is committed to a sustainable
future for our business, our readers and our planet.
This book is made from Forest Stewardship
Council™ certified paper.

ALWAYS LEARNING   **PEARSON**

CHAPTER ONE

'How are you feeling, Mary?' said Gran.

'I'm feeling fed up,' said Mary, and she slid down under the bedcovers.

'Careful! Watch your tray. Oh Mary, you've hardly touched that lovely bit of steamed plaice.'

Mary wrinkled her nose under the sheet. She hated steamed plaice, especially the pimply part.

'And you've left your rice pudding. Isn't there anything at all you fancy to eat, pet?' asked Gran.

Mary thought hard.

'I fancy chocolate. And crisps. And a can of coke.'

Gran snorted.

'That sort of junk's not going to make you better.'

'I *am* better,' said Mary. 'Dad said he didn't see why I couldn't go back to school today.'

'And Mummy said you're still a little chesty. You've had a nasty bout of flu, dear. We can't be too careful.'

Mary sighed. They were always so terribly careful. That was the trouble.

'Well, can't I even get up? I'm so bored of being in bed,' she grumbled.

'You need the rest, pet. You sound a bit overtired as it is. I do hope you're not getting feverish again. Let me take a good look at you.'

Gran pulled the sheets away from Mary's cross face and peered at her, feeling her forehead.

Mary fidgeted and fussed. She didn't like people staring at her. She hated the way she looked. She didn't like her round baby face and her long dark hair that always got into a tangle. But she could put up with that. It was her eyes she hated most.

Mum and Dad and Gran always said she had beautiful big brown eyes. Mary wasn't fooled. There was something odd about them. They stared in a strange way. People could tell straight away that she couldn't see properly.

She could see Gran bent right over her, her face all anxious lines. She could still see Gran when she stood up straight but the lines were wiped out, her face a blur.

When Gran moved round the bed to tuck in the rumpled bedcovers she stepped into a grey mist. The mist had been there ever since Mary was born.

'I think you'd better stay in bed for a bit,' said Gran's voice out of the mist.

Gran always liked to keep her in bed when she looked after her even when there was nothing whatever wrong. Gran worried that Mary might bump into things. Mum was almost as bad, following her from room to room and never letting her tackle the stairs by herself. And even Dad insisted on holding her hand when he took her to the park. It was as if she was stuck being a baby for ever just because she was nearly blind.

'I'll go and do the dishes and then bring you up a nice mug of hot milk,' said Gran. 'What would you like to do meanwhile? Read one of your story books?'

As long as she could hold the book right up close Mary could read anything. She wondered about *The Borrowers* or *Stuart Little* or one of her Anno picture books. No, maybe she felt like drawing her own picture. Although she'd dropped her big tin of felt-tip pens when she was crayoning in bed yesterday and she'd lost the special sky blue, her favourite colour. She could never find things when they rolled into dark corners, and Gran wasn't much better at it either.

'Can I have my scrapbook and that pile of magazines and the scissors?' said Mary.

'I don't think that's very sensible,' said Gran. 'I don't like the idea of you using scissors, Mary.'

'Oh Gran, I'm not stupid,' said Mary. 'I can manage scissors.'

'You have to put your face so near to

where you're cutting. I'm scared you'll jab the points right into your eyes.'

'I'm not a baby!'

'No, dear. Now, which story book shall it be?'

'I'm sick of reading. I'm sick of everything,' Mary moaned, flopping back on her pillow.

'Now who's acting like a baby?' said Gran, and went downstairs.

Mary lay on her back staring up into the blue above her. She knew her lampshade was there somewhere but she couldn't see it. She couldn't see the window. She couldn't see her bookshelf. She couldn't see her Sylvanian family country cottage. She couldn't see Little Ted or Middly Ted. She couldn't even see Great Big Ted at this distance though he was almost as big as she was.

Mary shut her eyes and put her hands

over her quivering eyelids. She still some-times pretended that she'd find some magic way of making her eyes see properly at last. Maybe if she counted to a certain number, or said the right combination of words, or bumped her head in a special way on the pillow . . .

But when she opened her eyes she was still stuck in her own strange world of half sight. Mum and Dad called her partially sighted. She didn't like the sound of that. It was as if she was only part of a proper person. Gran didn't call it anything at all, but she often lowered her voice and said The Poor Little Pet. Mary didn't want to be partial and she certainly didn't want to be a pet. She wanted to be a perfectly ordinary girl who could see properly.

She knew this wasn't possible. Her eyes were never going to get better. She'd had several operations but they hadn't helped much. The last operation had stopped her squinting, but when she went down the road with Mum the children playing on the pavement still called her Boss-Eyes, and when Mary got really close she thought they were making their own eyes squint, mocking her.

Mum said they were silly and ignorant and she wasn't to take any notice. Mary couldn't help noticing. She hated those children. Yet she couldn't help wishing she could go and play with them and be part of their little gang. She didn't have any friends who lived nearby. She had lots of friends at her special school but they all lived miles away so she couldn't often play with them after school.

Mary mostly had to play by herself. It got boring sometimes. She'd got very very bored having this stupid flu. Mum had stayed off work with her at first. Then Dad took a day off. And now Gran was looking after her and it was driving Mary mad.

'Here's your hot milk, pet,' said Gran, bustling back into Mary's bedroom.

'I don't really like hot milk, Gran.'

'Nonsense, dear. You need the nourishment. Drink it up while it's still warm. And then I think we'll settle you down for a little nap.'

Mary heard Gran arrange herself in the armchair and start her knitting. She was working on a new jumper for Mary. It was a dinky little pastel pink affair and Mary was not looking forward to wearing it. Gran's needles clicked busily for a minute or two. Mary had one sip of her milk. Gran's needles slowed down. Then they stopped altogether. Silence. And then Gran started snoring.

Mary put down her brimming mug of milk and sat up. She crawled to the end of

her bed and had a proper close-up peer at
Gran. She was definitely the one having
the little nap. Though it sounded more like
heavy slumber.

Mary sighed. She got back into bed
but she couldn't get comfortable. She
kicked at her covers. Her tummy rumbled.
She was so hungry. She felt carefully for
the mug of milk but it had a skin on it and
it made her shudder. She hated milk anyway. She longed for a long cold fizzy drink
of coke. And sharp savoury crackly crisps.
And smooth sweet creamy chocolate. Her
mouth was watering.

Maybe she could persuade Gran to go
down to the corner shop for coke and
crisps and chocolate when she woke up. It
was only a few seconds' walk away. But
Gran would never risk leaving her on her
own, not even if she promised to stay in
bed.

It was crazy. What on earth could happen to her? They always fussed so much when she could manage perfectly. She could go to the corner shop herself for that matter. She was just as capable as any other child. She'd been there and back hundreds of times with Mum.

So why couldn't she go to the shop by herself? Why *couldn't* she?

CHAPTER TWO

It was a mad idea.

Or was it?

'I could go to the shop by myself, easy-peasy,' Mary whispered.

It wouldn't take five minutes. She could slip out of the house and back, and Gran would never even know she'd gone.

'So why not?' said Mary.

She knew why not. Mum and Dad and Gran would faint at the very idea. But she couldn't help that. She was so sick of being a baby. She wanted to try something for herself. And she *knew* she could do it. She knew the way backwards. There weren't any roads to cross. No trees, no kerbs, no broken paving stones. She could go straight to the corner shop. There was just the one shop, a little grocery and post office, so she wouldn't get muddled and go in the wrong place.

She knew the man in the shop, Mr Soli. She knew Mrs Soli too. They were always gentle and friendly when she went in the shop with Mum. She could tell them what she wanted and they'd find the things for her and take the right money. And oh she did so want some coke and crisps and chocolate.

But what if Gran woke up while she was gone? What if she bumped into the things in the shop? What if there was a dog that jumped up at her? What if . . .?

'What if I go anyway, just this once, to see if I can,' Mary whispered, and she felt very carefully in her bedside cupboard for her purse.

She had a folded five pound note, several gold pound coins and lots of silver because she'd been saving for ages. She could buy a whole shop full of coke and crisps and chocolate and still have change.

So what else did she need besides money?

'Front door key! And shopping bag,' she said, nodding. She had to do things properly. It was no use getting all the way to the shop and back to find herself locked out of the house. And she'd need the shopping bag so that she could have one hand free to feel her way safely back.

She crept across the carpet and had another close peer at Gran. She was still fast asleep. She didn't even stir.

Mary waved her hand at her and then tiptoed out of the bedroom, clutching her purse. She slowed down out on the landing, her heart bumping hard in her chest. She felt slowly with her free hand for the banister rail. She found the edge of the stairs. She gripped the banister tightly and stepped down. One, two, three, four . . . it was easy now, she could just slide her hand down the banister railing, eight, nine, ten . . . nearly there, and she could still hear Gran snoring away . . . thirteen, fourteen, there, she'd made it, she was in the hall downstairs!

She felt cautiously for the hall table. Her fingers brushed the telephone and she jiggled the receiver, but she caught it in time. She felt across the table, down to the little drawer where she knew Mum kept the spare door key. She found it. She crept into the kitchen and found the shopping bag hanging from the door handle. There. She was all set.

She felt her way to the front door, opened it very slowly and cautiously so that it wouldn't make a noise, and then stepped out on to the garden path. It was quite cold and she shivered. Maybe she should put on a jacket?

'Oh help!' Mary gasped, suddenly remembering. Her hands scrabbled over her arms, her chest, her legs, feeling crumpled cotton. She was outdoors in her pyjamas!

She shot back inside, hoping no one had spotted her. She started giggling weakly at her own stupidity. Maybe she wasn't safe to be let out after all!

So what was she going to do about clothes? If she went all the way upstairs again and started raking around in her chest of drawers then Gran was bound to wake up. Wait a minute. She tried the kitchen. There weren't any clothes on the airer, but there was a plastic basket of ironing in the corner. Mary felt amongst the folded clothes to find something that fitted. She couldn't very well go out in Dad's shirt or Mum's skirt. She found her own T-shirt, her own jeans. She didn't care if they looked a bit creased.

She was still stuck for shoes, but then she remembered her wellingtons that were in their usual corner by the back door. They'd do. She was ready.

Or was she? Where was the shopping bag, with her purse and key?

'Oh no,' said Mary, peering desperately, trying to see its dark shape.

She blundered up and down the hall, crouched over, feeling for the bag.

'Where *are* you?' she whispered, and then she stumbled right over it.

She couldn't help crying out. She stayed still, her hand over her mouth, listening. She waited for Gran to call for her. But she was all right after all. She could faintly hear Gran's soft steady snoring as she slept on undisturbed.

Mary opened the front door and stepped out. She closed the door behind her as quietly as she could, took a deep breath, and then walked slowly down her garden path. It was edged with little bricks so she could tell exactly where she was going. She got to the garden gate and opened it easily enough. She walked out on the pavement and then stood still for a moment, smiling triumphantly. It was the first time she'd ever been out alone.

She took another deep breath and set off up the road. She felt with her right hand for the hedge, then the metal gate, then the next hedge, then a wooden gate, a little brick wall, and then – help! Something warm, something hairy! Someone's head poking over the wall?

'I'm sorry,' she mumbled, hot with horror.

The head stalked away with an indignant miaow.

Mary giggled.

'Here, puss,' she called, edging along the wall.

She caught the cat up and got close enough to see it properly.

'Hello, little cat,' she said, stroking it under its chin. 'You didn't half give me a fright.'

The cat allowed itself to be stroked. It started to purr. Mary was enchanted. She didn't come across many animals at close quarters. She'd always longed for a cat or a dog, but Mum thought she'd be forever tripping over it. It wasn't fair. Mary was only clumsy because she couldn't see properly, not because she was stupid or careless. She felt particularly competent right this moment, out of doors all by herself, making friends with a cat and doing her own shopping.

'Wait for me here, little cat. I'll just be two minutes down at the shop,' said Mary.

She carried on walking, counting the houses in her head. Only three more left. Two more. One. Now she was right outside Mr Soli's shop.

'Look, it's old Baby Boss-Eyes.'

'So it is! Pull a face at her, go on. She's blind as a bat, she can't see you.'

She could see a bit. She was close enough to see that one was a boy and one was a girl. Their faces were blurs but she didn't need sharp eyes to work out their expressions.

Mary stood still, right in front of them. She pulled her eyelids down. She pushed her nose up. She waggled her tongue to its fullest extent.

There was a little shocked silence and then the girl giggled.

'She can see after all. She pulled a face back.'

'No, she can't. Her eyes are all funny. She's blind, I tell you.'

'I'm *not* blind,' said Mary. 'I just can't see very much. Which suits me OK, because who'd want to look at a pair of twits like you?'

'Ooh, get her,' said the boy, but he sounded slightly impressed.

'Where's your mum then?' said the girl. 'I thought you weren't allowed out without your mum?'

'Who cares about my mum?' said Mary.

'Where are you going then?'

'The shop.'

'Is it your lunch break? You go to that special school, don't you? Where all the nuts and freaks go.'

'Sounds like you've got your fair share of nuts and freaks at your school. Judging by you two.'

'Shut-up, Boss-Eyes.'

'Look, my eyes might be funny, but they're not boss or cross or anything, so shut up calling me that.'

'What's your name then?' said the girl.

'Mary.'

'OK. I'll call you Mary. I'm Sue and this is Mick. Come on, we've got to get back to school. See you, Mary.'

'See you,' said Mary.

She waved in their direction and she thought they waved back, though she couldn't be sure. She was so pleased with herself she forgot to be cautious going into the shop and barged right into some wire baskets, banging her knee.

'Oh dear, are you all right, miss?' came Mr Soli's voice from behind his post office cage.

Mrs Soli rustled from behind the food counter. She seemed to have two faces, but when she was near enough to rub the sore knee Mary could see she was carrying a little Soli on her hip.

'It's OK, really, it doesn't even hurt,' said Mary. 'Can I have a can of coke, please? And a packet of crisps – salt and vinegar, I think. And I want some chocolate.'

'Chocolate is this way, on the counter. I'll show you,' said Mrs Soli, gently leading Mary by the elbow.

She held up bar after bar right in front of Mary's eyes so that she could see what was on offer. The baby Soli did his best to grab for the chocolate, making them all laugh. An old lady came into the shop for a loaf of bread.

'I've left my specs at home,' she said to Mary. 'Have I got the right packet, dear? Small sliced wholemeal?'

Mary laughed at the idea of anyone asking her to look for them.

'This little girl can't see so well herself,' said Mrs Soli.

'I can a bit,' said Mary, and she brought the packet of bread right in front of her eyes. 'Yes, that's a small sliced wholemeal,' she said proudly.

She still couldn't decide whether she wanted a Mars or a Kit Kat. Well, why not have both, seeing as this was such a special day?

She paid for the coke, crisps and the two bars of chocolate.

'You are a clever girl, managing so

well,' said the old lady with the bread.

'Shall I help you out of the door, dear?' said Mrs Soli.

'No, thank you, I can manage,' said Mary.

'Well, mind those baskets,' Mr Soli called.

'I'm minding them,' said Mary, moving cautiously forward towards the door.

And then she was knocked right over by two people rushing madly into the shop. She went sprawling on the floor, dropping her coke and crisps and chocolate.

'Watch the little girl!' Mrs Soli cried indignantly.

'Don't move! This is a hold-up!' a man shouted.

The other man pushed past Mary. He was close enough for her to see the long knife in his hand.

CHAPTER THREE

Mary crouched on the floor, terrified. She couldn't see what was going on, but she could hear.

'Hand over the money!' one man shouted, banging on the post office counter.

The other man had got Mrs Soli over by the window. He took hold of her by the hair. She cried out in her own language, and Mr Soli answered her.

'Don't jabber like that!' the man

shouted. 'Don't play games with us. And you can leave that alarm bell alone. One stupid move and we'll hurt your wife and kid.'

The baby Soli started wailing in a high-pitched panicky way, as if he understood.

Mary crouched down even smaller, wanting to cry too. The old lady with the wholemeal bread was stumbling about, making little whimpering noises.

'You there! Keep still and shut up,' the man shouted. 'Come on, give us the money. All of it. Don't try messing with us.'

'I'll give you all the money. Just don't hurt anybody. Get away from my wife, my baby. You're frightening them.'

'We give the orders round here. Now hurry!'

Hurry! Mary begged silently, her head almost on the floor.

She still couldn't believe it was actually happening. One minute she'd been so happy and proud and confident, buying chocolate at the corner shop like any other girl. And the next minute she was part of this nightmare robbery, and it was all so quick, so cruel, so frightening.

'Hurry him up!' the man called from the window. 'There's kids running round outside. They look as if they're up to something. Quick!'

'Hear that? Hand it all over now or I'm telling you, your wife gets it, and your kid.'

'Here! This is all, I swear. Take it. But for pity's sake, don't hurt anyone,' said Mr Soli desperately.

The baby cried harder. Mary clenched her fists so tightly her nails dug into her palms.

The other man suddenly swore. 'Those

kids, they've fetched the copper from the school crossing. Come on, mate, we've got to get out of here!'

'Right, here's the cash. Quick, catch! Let's go.'

'The copper! He's coming, he's coming!'

The man with the knife started running. Mary cowered away from him. He seemed to have a strange green face that made him even more frightening. He suddenly stopped, reached down and grabbed her by the shoulder.

'Get up, kid.'

'No!' Mary whispered.

'Just do as you're told,' said the man, and he yanked her to her feet. He thrust the knife right in her face. 'No silly tricks now. Come on, move it.'

He pushed her and she blundered helplessly, knocking into the shelves. The man grabbed her round the chest and hauled her along so quickly that the tips of her boots barely scuffed the floor.

'Leave the poor kid alone!' the old woman shouted, and she tried to waddle after them.

'Get out the way, you silly old bag,' yelled the other man.

He must have given her a push because the old woman grunted and then hit the floor with a bump. There was a series of soft thuds as a pile of toilet rolls fell on top of her. The man stumbled through them and got to the door. Then he yelled as a big burly shape loomed up. There was a bang, more thuds, and a gasp for help as they struggled.

'Leave him, copper!' shouted Mary's man. 'Let him go or the kid gets it.'

The scuffling stopped. The two indistinct figures seemed to freeze.

'Now, come on, lads. I've put a call out, the place will be crawling with police by now. There's no point in any silly stuff. Let the little girl go.'

'Oh no! She's coming with us. And you'd better stand out of our way or she'll get cut.'

He waved the knife wildly and then stuck the blade right under Mary's chin, so close she could feel the cold steel.

'All right! All right, just don't hurt her,' the policeman called.

'Let my mate go.'

'OK. There. See, he's free now.'

'Come on, quick!' yelled Mary's man, and he picked her right up and ran with her. The knife bobbed up and down in front of her and she stared at the terrible gleam of it.

There were shouts and gasps and running feet. She was suspended helplessly, not daring to move or speak or even cry, not while the knife was an inch from her face.

'What are we going to do?' gasped the other man.

'We're going to get out of here, that's what we're going to do,' Mary's man panted. 'The car, let's get in the car.'

They ran wildly across the road, although the man was gasping for breath now and his grip wasn't as tight. As he got across the road he tripped on the kerb and very nearly dropped Mary. She tensed, ready for the sharp slap of the pavement, desperately determined to run for it no matter how much it hurt.

But it was no use. He clutched at her, the knife slipping for a moment, but then he clasped it again, and he had Mary in a new fierce grip too, her head jerked right back.

'Get the car, get the door open, get it going!' he gabbled to his friend.

He stayed still, one leg up against the car to take some of the weight. His arm was so hard against her throat she could hardly swallow. The hairs on his arm were standing out. There were ugly blue tattoos patterning his skin: a skull and crossbones, a snake winding right round his wrist, and a distorted gorilla beating its chest.

There was a bang from the other side of the car. The friend had got the door open, was in, starting up the engine. He had a green face too, another alien.

'Right,' said the man with the knife, grappling with his own door, jerking Mary up and down. The skull and the snake and the gorilla danced crazily in and out of Mary's vision but the knife stayed steely still, constantly before her eyes.

'What you doing?' the other man said.

'Come on, drop the kid and we'll get out of here.'

Yes, drop me, drop me, please drop me! Mary begged inside her head.

'Oh no, the kid's coming with us,' said the man with the knife, and he pushed Mary into the car and got in after her.

'Are you crazy?' the other man said.

'Just start the car and get us out of here.'

'OK, OK, but I'm telling you, you've flipped your lid. You can't take the kid. There'll be thousands of coppers after us if we take the kid.'

'They're after us anyway. She's our insurance. The kid stays with us.'

Chapter Four

'Please,' Mary begged, but the man with the knife pressed her down on to the floor of the car.

'Keep still and shut up,' he said.

Mary couldn't see the knife any more but she knew it was there. She had to do as she was told.

The car swerved violently round a corner and hurtled forward. Then the brakes were slammed suddenly and the man swore.

'Out of the way, you fool!' the driver shouted.

'Drive through them, Micky. Come on, the police might be right on our back.'

The car took off again, swerving, screeching, almost out of control. Mary juddered up and down on the dusty floor. She started to feel sick. Tears rolled down her cheeks. She wanted her mum, her dad, her gran.

If only she'd stayed tucked up in bed at home! It was so unfair. If these hateful robbers hadn't come along she'd have managed perfectly. She'd got to the shop all by herself. She'd have got back again, no bother, and she'd be tucking into her coke and crisps and chocolate right this minute. Gran would still be snoring away none the wiser.

But what would happen now when she woke up? She'd hunt the house for Mary and then phone Mum, phone Dad, out of her mind with worry.

They'll be so cross with me when I get back, thought Mary. And then she had another thought. A worse one. What if I don't ever get back?

It was as if someone had thrown icy water all over her, making her shiver. But it cleared her head a little.

I've *got* to get back, she thought. She looked at the dirty trainers in front of her face. She was going to get away from this horrible man somehow. She was going to get back to Mum and Dad and Gran. So she had to be as clever as she could. She had to try to work out where they were taking her.

How long had they been driving? Time seemed to have gone crazy. It seemed hours and hours since the robbers burst into the corner shop but that couldn't be right. They'd only been driving a few minutes. That meant they were still pretty close to home.

Mary was used to riding around in cars. She was driven to her special school and back every day. On Saturdays Dad drove them to the big supermarket. On Sundays they often went for a drive into the countryside. Mary could never just peer out the window to see where they were going. She could only see a blur of moving shapes. But she'd worked out all sorts of ways of guessing where they were. So now it was time to start concentrating properly.

The car suddenly veered right round, making Mary's tummy churn. That was a roundabout. And then there was a new vibration as they sped along a different road surface. Simple. They were going along the bypass. And then after a few minutes they veered to the left. Was that the turning Dad took when they were going to the supermarket? They'd maybe have to slow down soon because there were often queues of cars trying to turn into the supermarket car-park.

'Come on!' yelled the driver, sounding his horn.

Mary gritted her teeth triumphantly. She was right. She knew exactly where they were.

'Overtake them!' the knife man shouted.

'How can I? There's no room.'

'Listen. Is that a police siren?'

'It is! OK, sit tight.'

The car shot forward, weaving wildly. There was a sudden bump, a scraping sound, furious hooting horns, but the car didn't stop. It was going at such a crazy speed that the floor vibrated violently. Mary moaned to get up but the man had his hand on her back, holding her down.

You pig, she thought. She felt sicker than ever. She was getting bumped and bruised, and her knees were sore anyway from falling over in the shop. But she was tougher than anyone thought. She often fell over things so she was used to bits hurting. She wasn't going to let them distract her. She had to keep on thinking where they were going so that somehow she'd be able to find her way back.

The car shot off to the right, rocketing up on the pavement and down again, jerking them about.

'Watch it!' shouted the knife man.

'That's what I'm trying to do!'

The siren wailed.

'Just get a move on. Quick!'

'We can't go any quicker. What are we going to do? They're getting nearer!'

Yes, come on, get nearer. Come and

catch them, Mary urged inside her head. Rescue me!

The man's hand pressed hard on her back.

'We've got the kid. They can't try anything too clever, not when we've got her.'

Mary's tummy lurched. What would they do to her if the police tried to ambush them?

Help! Mary shouted silently.

The siren wailed continuously, getting nearer now.

'Move it!' the knife man shouted, craning round to see out of the back window.

Then he gave a weird yelp of laughter.

'It's not a police car at all, it's an ambulance. We've been scared witless by an ambulance!'

'It's me that'll be needing an ambulance soon,' said the driver, 'the way my heart's pounding.'

'Never mind your heart. Just use your head. We've still got to get clear. I don't know if that copper read the number plate of the car or not. They could still be after us. So come on, make for the flat, sharpish. But take the balaclava off now, try and look natural.'

The knife man peeled off his own balaclava and dropped it down beside Mary. She peered at the green wool and understood the strange faces. But they were still acting like aliens.

'Why does it have to be my flat?'

'It's nearest.'

'Why can't we go to your place?'

'Just drive, will you! I'll make the decisions.'

'What about the kid? How's she doing down there? She is all right? You haven't hurt her?'

'You'll be the one to get hurt if you don't

shut up and concentrate on getting us out of here!'

Mary was trying hard to concentrate too. She tried to sort out all the roads in her head, but she'd got in a bit of a muddle. They turned left, and left again . . . She was lost now. She tried to remember the left and right turns but there were too many. How would she ever find her way back?

They suddenly swerved to a halt.

'Don't park right outside, you berk! Put the car round the back and shove some tarpaulins over it. We don't want to take any chances,' said the knife man.

The car was driven slowly down an alleyway. The man switched off the engine. There was a sudden silence.

'Well, we made it!' said the knife man.

'Maybe,' said the driver. 'I still don't like it. It all turned ugly – and it was a mistake getting the kid involved.'

'Oh shut up. If it hadn't been for the kid we'd never have got you away.'

'Anyway, better let her toddle off now,' said the driver, leaning over his seat. 'You all right, kid?' he asked Mary.

She gave a little gulp.

'What are you playing at, Bob, squashing her down on the floor like that? Come on, Tuppenny, out you come.'

'Leave her be. I'll see to her. We didn't want her seeing where we were going, did we?'

'Come off it. She doesn't have a clue where she is. She's only little. Look at her face, she's been crying. Don't you fret, kid, we'll get you back to your mum now.'

'No. We're keeping her.'

Mary quivered.

'Are you mad? Robbing post offices not enough for you? Going in for kidnapping now? You fancy doing a ten- or twenty-year stretch in the nick?'

'We'll keep her just for a bit. In case the coppers trace the car and come nosing round here.'

'We can't keep her! Look at her, she's doing her nut as it is. Here, dry your eyes, girlie,' he said, offering her a rag. 'What's up with them, eh? They look all funny.'

Mary sniffed and scrubbed at her face with the cloth.

'We can't keep her, Bob.'

'Will you shut it? We don't want her blabbing our names to the coppers, do we?'

'Well, why keep her hanging round us any longer? She's copping a good look at us, isn't she?'

'Oh no she's not!' said the knife man, snatching the cloth away from Mary's face and staring at her. 'Take a good look at

her. She's useless as a witness. What a
piece of luck! She can't see. She's blind as
a bat!'

CHAPTER FIVE

Mary always hated being called blind. It wasn't true for a start. She *could* see, even if it was only a few inches in front of her face. But she had enough sense to keep her mouth shut now.

The hateful knife man waved his hand in front of her face. The knife went horribly near her nose but Mary managed not to flinch.

'See that? You're blind, aren't you, kid?

47

So you don't have a clue who we are or what we look like, that's right, isn't it?'

Mary nodded. It wasn't true. She was adding up all sorts of things about the man inside her head.

'Let's get her indoors quick. Give us the keys, Micky. And the money. You deal with the car. I'd get those number plates changed, sharpish. Or nick another car.'

He gave Mary a tug, and opened the car door.

'Come on, kid, get moving.'

Mary had been cramped up for so long it was a hard job to move at all. Pins and needles prickled her legs, so that she hobbled and nearly fell as he dragged her out. The fresh air in the backyard smelt good after the stuffy car. She turned her head, trying desperately to see just a little. Her eyes watered with the strain. Were those dark shapes houses? If they were houses then they'd have people inside them. People who might help her.

She filled her lungs with air. What if she screamed for help at the top of her voice and then tried to run for it?

But the knife man was still holding on to her. He pulled her close to him, the knife at her back now. The bulky money bag bumped against her legs.

'No funny business, kid, do you hear? One squeak out of you and you'll get it.'

Mary nodded silently, knowing she'd better do as he said. The man pulled her over towards the shadow of the house. She didn't know which way to go and the pins and needles were still hurting her legs. She stumbled and he shook her impatiently.

'Walk properly!'

Mary's eyes stung. He was so mean and cruel and unfair. She wanted to shout all sorts of things at him but she didn't dare, not with the knife at her back.

He pulled her along until they came to some steps with a railing. Mary froze, terrified of tripping again.

'Move it!'

Mary moved, and very nearly fell head-long. The steps didn't go up as she'd expected. They went *down*. She couldn't understand it. If you were on the ground then steps always went up, didn't they? But these definitely went down to a dank cold little landing. The man fiddled with the keys and then pushed her inside.

Mary's boots squeaked on the floor. She must be in a kitchen. Her nose wrinkled at the smell of sour dishcloths and unemptied rubbish.

'What a tip,' the man muttered, and he pushed Mary through the first room and into a second.

He left her where she was while he went and swished the curtains, closing them all. Then there was a click from a corner of the room and a sudden burst of talking, making her start. He'd obviously switched on the television.

'Out the way, kid, you're in front of the screen.'

Mary ducked first to one side, then the other, not knowing where to go. She tripped over some sort of footstool and fell on her hands and knees. The man laughed as if she'd done something funny.

'Blind as a bat!'

Mary stifled a sob. She sat where she was, not daring to move any more. She heard the man opening a cupboard door and then a little hiss as he opened a can of drink. The television blared uncomfortably loudly.

'Oh fine, make yourself at home,' said

the other man, coming into the room. 'What you closed the curtains for? It's broad daylight.'

'Exactly. We don't want anyone peering down into your mucky little dungeon and spotting the kid, do we? How often do you clean this dump, Micky? It's filthy. And that smell, it's turning my stomach.'

'Oh pardon me I'm sure. I wasn't expecting to do any entertaining. I see you've helped yourself to a drink already.'

'Yeah, and you can get us some food too, I'm starving.'

'I thought you felt sick? I blooming well do. And switch that television off, I've got a headache.'

'I want to catch the news. We might be on it.'

'Are you mad? You're sounding as if you're enjoying all this!'

'Well, why not? We got the money,

didn't we? Look at it all. And we got away with it too.'

'We got away with the *kid*.' He came closer and bent down right in front of Mary. She still couldn't see his face properly. She didn't dare try to focus in case he'd notice. She kept her eyes deliberately vague, swivelling from side to side. Tears were still dribbling down her cheeks.

'Look at her! It's all right, pet, we'll be letting you go home to your mummy very soon.'

Mary thought of Mum and cried harder.

'Can't you stop the kid snivelling? It's getting on my nerves,' said the knife man. He was rustling paper, muttering, counting. 'We got away with quite a bundle, Micky. More than we hoped for. And yet . . . I don't know. It doesn't seem so much when you think of the risks we took.'

'Yeah, quite! So maybe we should cool it for a bit.'

'Or maybe . . . maybe we should go for the big time number. Start talking in thousands. Maybe a hundred thousand, maybe even more.'

'What you on about? You flipped your lid with all the excitement?' said Micky, coming back to Mary. 'Here, kid. Like crisps? Have some of these. Can you feed yourself or do you want me to do it for you?'

'I can do it,' Mary whispered, marvelling at his stupidity. But at least he wasn't as nasty as the other one.

'Give us some crisps, Micky. And anything else you've got. I tell you I'm starving. And I'm not off my head. I reckon we're on to a sure thing. We'll ransom the kid.'

Mary choked on a crisp. The hard edge

scratched her throat. She sat still with her mouth full of softening salty crisps, barely able to swallow.

'You *are* mad! Look, mate, I'm not getting into any kidnapping game, I'm telling you. I'm strictly for the small-time.'

'But we're big-time now whether you like it or not,' said the knife man, springing across the room to turn the television up again. 'Look!'

Mary couldn't look but she could listen.

'A disturbing news item has just come in about a post office robbery in Kingston, in which the two robbers abducted a little blind girl. We'll hope to have more on that story in our next bulletin,' said the television announcer.

'Oh no!' said Micky. 'You idiot, I knew taking the kid was a mistake. Look at us now. Right on the main news!'

'You'd be banged up in the local nick right this minute if we hadn't taken the kid.'

'Yeah, well, maybe that would have been better than this. They'll have half the coppers in the country out after us. We'd better let the kid go now, Bob.'

'Oh yeah? And how you going to do that, eh? Escort her down the road and wave bye-bye to her outside the local cop shop?'

'Well, of course not. But we could . . . we could take her out in the car some-where –'

'When the whole manor's buzzing with cops? Very sensible.'

'Yeah well, maybe tonight then, after dark . . .'

'Think they'll let up then? They'll nab us as soon as we're down the street, and you know it. I reckon the kid will be headline news by the next bulletin, specially as she's blind. They'll have a description of her. She'll be dynamite.'

'So what the hell are we going to do?' said Micky, his voice high with panic.

Mary surreptitiously spat out her soggy mouthful of crisps, and waited.

'I'm *telling* you. We'll keep her. Make no move for several days, so that her parents get nice and desperate. And then we'll make contact and ask for the money. Big money.'

Several days! Mary thought in agony.

'She's just an ordinary kid. It's not like she's a millionaire's kid. You're off your head, man. How can they ever raise that sort of cash?'

'That's their problem. They've got a house, haven't they? So they can think about flogging it. Hey, kid, what sort of house do you live in?'

Mary shook her head, not knowing what to say.

'Is it a big house?' Micky asked more gently.

'Mmm,' said Mary.

'And what does your dad do for a living, eh?'

'He goes out to business,' Mary whispered.

'There, a businessman! Maybe he's one of these city types, worth a fortune,' said the knife man triumphantly.

'But what if he isn't? What if they can't get the cash?' Micky asked.

'Then they can't get the kid back, can they?' said the knife man.

Mary shivered.

'I don't like it, Bob. It's much too risky. How are you going to make contact? And if they come up with the cash, how are you going to hand over the kid without the cops leaping up and down on you?'

'We'll work out the details later. We've got plenty of time. Meanwhile let's just take it easy.' He opened another can of drink.

Mary's dry throat tried to swallow on nothing.

'Please,' she whispered. 'Please could I have a drink too?'

'Sure thing, kid,' said the knife man, and threw a can at her, laughing.

'No,' said Micky snatching it away from her. 'No, you don't want that, kid, it's beer. I'll get you something. What do you like drinking, eh? What do kids drink? I think all the milk's gone sour.'

'Like everything else in this dump. Go out down the shops, Micky, get some drinks in, and some Chinese take-aways.'

'I can't go *out*, it's too risky. What if they got a good description of us?'

'We had the balaclavas on, didn't we? So what could they see? Two blokes in jeans. We could be anybody. Don't start getting so windy, Micky. You've got to act natural. Go about your usual business so none of your neighbours twig there's anything suspicious.'

'Oh sure. And what if they hear the kid crying, what then?'

'We'll put a gag on her.'

'I won't cry!' said Mary quickly.

She wanted to cry so much. It got worse when Micky went out for food and drink. Mary was left alone with the knife man.

Chapter Six

Mary sat hunched in her corner, tense and still. The knife man was too far away for her to see anything but a dark shape. He was sitting still too. She was scared he was watching her.

Every so often he raised his can of drink and swallowed steadily. If only he'd go on drinking and get really drunk so that he'd fall asleep. Then she could run away. She couldn't stand the thought of staying shut up with these horrible men day after day. Especially the knife man.

She heard the chair creak as he stood up. He came padding towards her in his soft trainers. He squatted down in front of her, so that she could see his face properly. It was like a white mask. His cold eyes flickered from side to side as he stared at her. He had his knife in his hand.

Mary started to shiver.

The man tapped the knife against his knee in a slow insistent way.

'What am I going to do with you, kid?' he muttered. 'Are you going to be worth all the bother and risk?'

Mary stayed still, struggling not to cry.

Then she heard the key in the door. Micky was back.

'What are you up to, Bob?' he asked uneasily.

'I've just been doing a little pondering,'

said the knife man. 'Is that more beer? And some grub?'

'Yeah, hang on, let me get it all organized. I didn't half feel weird down the shops. Everyone was talking about the robbery and the blind kid. I had to join in, say it was a shame. Oh boy. I was sweating like a pig. You can go out for the grub next, Bob.'

He bustled around with the cartons of food.

'Here, kid. You like sweet and sour pork and rice? I'll get you a spoon. I've got you some coke to drink. You like that, don't you? And some chocolate for pudding, eh?'

'Stop fussing round her like a mother hen,' said the knife man. 'She don't need all that.'

'Look, we've already frightened the poor little kid half to death. I'm not starving her to death too,' said Micky.

'I said quit fussing.'

'Who are you to give me orders?' said Micky.

They both stood up. Mary crouched down low, scared they were going to start fighting. But a television news bulletin started and they were all distracted.

This time there was a film of the post office. Mary couldn't see the screen at all but she heard both Mr and Mrs Soli talking worriedly, telling about the robbery. They even had the old wholemeal bread lady saying how awful it was, and how she felt sorry for the poor little kiddie.

That's me! thought Mary. They were talking about her on television.

'Just a little scrap of a thing. Six or seven, not any older,' said the old lady.

I'm nine! thought Mary indignantly.

'And totally blind,' said the old lady.

I could tell you which bread to get! thought Mary.

'The police are conducting a massive search for the post office robbers and the missing child,' said the television announcer.

'Phew!' said Micky shakily, when the announcer switched to another subject. 'You're right, Bob. It's big time now, whether we like it or not.'

'Smack on the national news. And we've carried it off! They don't have a clue who we are and they don't know where the kid is. So we're OK for now, like I keep telling you,' said the knife man, opening another beer and rustling in the paper carton for his Chinese meal.

Micky fetched Mary a spoon and she did her best to eat although she was still too scared to feel hungry. She drank all her coke though, gulping it down until the can was empty. It tasted wonderful, but ever since the robbery she'd been needing to go to the lavatory and now she became desperate.

'Please,' she said to Micky.

'You what?'

Mary struggled to get the words out. She hated having to ask him but she was worried about wetting herself like a baby.

'Oh, I get you. Come on then, I'll take you,' said Micky.

He took her by the hand and carefully steered her round a table and past a chair.

'Just you keep an eye on her, Mary Poppins,' said the knife man, but he sounded more relaxed now.

Mary worried that Micky would come right into the bathroom with her, but he waited outside the door.

I should try to get away right now, thought Mary. Maybe it's my only chance.

She used the lavatory first and then stood up on the seat. There was a window. It was only a very small one but she was a very small girl. Maybe she could squeeze right through.

'Are you OK in there?' Micky called.

'Mmm,' Mary mumbled.

She felt the window frame, found the handle. But then she heard the door open and she staggered back, very nearly falling right into the lavatory.

'What on earth are you up to?' Micky said, catching hold of her.

'I – I was – I was trying to find the chain to pull it,' Mary stammered.

'Oh. Well, I'll do it for you. There we go,' said Micky, and then he lifted her down.

The chance was gone.

He led her back into the main room and sat her in a chair.

'Cheer up,' he said. 'What's that long face for? I got you some nice food and drink, didn't I? Here, you haven't had your chocolate.'

Mary ate a square and choked. She started a coughing fit.

'Stop that row,' said the knife man.

Mary tried hard. But she'd just had flu and couldn't help having a cough.

'Right. We'll put that gag on her,' said the knife man.

'Here, have another coke,' said Micky. 'She don't need no gag, Bob. She just needs another drink, that's all.'

Mary drank. It helped a little. Her throat still tickled unbearably and her chest was tight, but she clamped her lips together. She spluttered a little but she didn't cough.

'There, that's better,' said Micky.

He sat beside her and chatted for a bit,

but he soon got bored. He was drinking a lot of beer too. After a while his voice started to slur. Mary sat still, her hand over her mouth in case she coughed again. They were really getting drunk now. Maybe she still had a chance to run away.

Micky slumped down beside the chair. His slow steady breathing soon became snores. Mary listened hard for any sounds coming from the man with the knife. He stayed silent. He could be asleep too, but she couldn't be sure.

She had a horrible feeling that he was still watching her.

CHAPTER SEVEN

Mary sat still and waited. She waited
and waited. She was still scared but she
was getting so bored too. The television
was on but she couldn't work out what was
happening. She didn't have anything at
all to play with. It was so hard to be
expected to sit still and do nothing at
all for hours on end. She tried twiddling
her thumbs, twining her fingers, waggling
her hands. She pretended they were two

spiders and made them go for walks up and down her legs.

'Quit that fiddling, it's getting on my nerves,' said the knife man, making her jump.

No, he wasn't asleep. He was still wide awake, watching. Mary sat on her hands to stop them fidgeting. She tried to think of things to do inside her head. She counted up to one hundred. Five hundred. All the way up to a thousand. She thought of all the songs she knew and sang them inside her head. She thought of all her favourite things and made lists of them. She thought of Mum and Dad and Gran . . . and that was a mistake.

Tears dripped down her cheeks. She struggled hard but she couldn't help sniffling.

'Stop that,' said the knife man.

She covered her face with her fingers.

She cried silently behind her hands until she fell asleep. She had a lot of nightmares. The worst was dreaming two hateful robbers had taken her prisoner. She woke up feeling very frightened.

It's all right. It was only a silly dream, she told herself.

Then she heard the blaring television, the hiss of another beer can being opened – and remembered. The dream was real.

'The kid's awake,' said Micky. His voice was so slurred now she could hardly understand what he was saying. 'You missed out on supper, kid. Fish and chips. There's still a few chips somewhere. Want some?'

Mary felt too sick and scared to eat. She huddled in a small ball, sucking her thumb.

The television was very loud. There was creepy music and then sudden screams. Micky laughed and the knife man snorted several times. They were obviously watching some horror video.

Mary felt as if she was taking part in her own horror movie. If only she could fast forward herself to the end of the tape and safety!

'Want a drink?' Micky asked.

'Please,' said Mary.

She was careful to take just a few sips, although she was still very thirsty. She waited a while, trying to think things out in her head.

Then she swallowed, cleared her throat nervously and spoke to Micky.

'Will you take me to the bathroom again, please?'

He groaned, but got to his feet willingly enough. He wasn't so good at leading her this time. Mary unwittingly blundered against the chair where the knife man was sitting.

'Watch my drink, kid,' he said sharply.

'Whoopsie-daisy,' said Micky, staggering.

'Stupid drunken sot,' the knife man muttered. 'Keep your eye on that kid, do you hear?'

'Yes, Boss. Sure thing, Boss. Three bags full, Boss.' Micky giggled stupidly.

'We'll have to tie her to the chair for the night. We can't take any chances on her making a run for it when we're having a kip.'

'Easy, Bob. She's not much more than a baby. As if a kid like that could make a run for it,' said Micky.

Mary said nothing. Micky staggered out with her to the bathroom.

'There you go, kid,' he said, and he pushed her gently forward into the room.

This time she felt for the lock on the door and very cautiously slotted it into place. Then she was up on top of the lavatory seat and feeling for the handle of the window. She jiggled the handle but nothing happened. She screwed up her face in desperation and tried again, shoving hard at the stiff window – and at the third thud it juddered open. Mary stood right up on tiptoe and thrust her arm out into thin air. Then her shoulder and head. Her free hand found a ledge to cling to. She gripped it as hard as she could and then heaved. Somehow she got her bottom up on to the window-ledge. It was easy now to pull her legs up and squat outside. Now all she had to do was jump.

Only she couldn't see a thing. It had got dark outside, blacking out the little vision she had left. How could she jump when she didn't know how far down it was? She remembered the weird steps going down and the little landing. If she was above the little landing then that was easy. It was only a hop or two to the ground. But what if there were more steps somehow, leading further down? She was frantic to get away from Micky and the knife man but she didn't want to break her neck in the process.

She felt a pebble on the crumbling ledge. She dropped it and listened. It landed with a ping in less than a second. She was O K. Or was she?

'Here, kid! What are you up to?' Micky's voice called faintly.

She had to jump and hope for the best. She stepped out into the blackness, fell forwards and landed with a great clang on top of a dustbin. She felt as if she'd been punched in the stomach and lay still, shivering in the cold evening air.

'Kid! Let me in! What are you playing at

in there?' Micky's voice was angry. She heard the thud as his shoulder hit the bathroom door.

She had to get moving. She wriggled off the dustbin, and blundered forward, arms outstretched. She found another dustbin, and then a space. She risked running, and tripped, something sharp biting her shins. She bent and felt with her hands. The steps!

She heard a crash inside. Micky had obviously broken down the door. With a little gasp Mary scampered on all fours up the steps. 'Quick! She's got out of the window! After her!' Micky yelled.

Mary went on scrabbling up the steps, trying to go faster, but it was so hard when she couldn't see where she was going. Just one stumble could send her somersaulting down the whole flight.

She heard the outside door open and

swift purposeful footsteps. The man with the knife was after her!

Mary missed the step, nearly tripped – but somehow managed to keep her footing. She carried on climbing, gasping for breath, but the steps seemed to stretch on for ever.

Chapter Eight

The man with the knife was getting closer.
She could hear his feet pounding across the
landing towards the steps, getting nearer
and nearer . . .

Then there was a crash, a shout,
muttered swearing. He'd blundered right
into the dustbin! He was almost as helpless
as she was in the dark!

Mary heard him moaning and cursing
as he tried to stand. Had he hurt himself?

She staggered on up the steps, flung out her arms, and felt the railings. She was at the top at last. She gripped the peeling paint, gasping for breath. Now, what next?

What sort of street was she in? She couldn't hear any traffic or see a blur of bright lights. It seemed to be a deserted back street. She had to get moving quickly. If the man with the knife or Micky caught up with her here then she'd have no chance.

She started running down the street. Were they after her? She kept looking behind even though she knew she couldn't possibly see. She ran with one arm feeling in front and one arm waving feebly behind her, trying to feel if they were catching her. It didn't help her keep her balance and she stumbled several times, twisting her ankle, but she didn't dare stop. She didn't even stop when she tripped right off the

kerb and realized she'd got to the end of
the little street. She turned the corner in
the gutter, found the pavement again, and
ran on. Her flailing arm caught hold of a
lamppost but she ran round it in time,
though her fingers throbbed with the
impact.

She was starting to hurt all over, and she
was coughing now, hardly able to get her
breath. She knew she couldn't go on running much longer. They were going to
catch her up any second.

She had to find someone to help her.
There were lights in this big street and
lights meant people. She veered towards
them and when she was right up close she
saw they were shop windows. But when
she found a door and pushed at it frantic-
ally it wouldn't open. The shop was shut,
and so was the next one and the next.

'Please!' Mary gasped, hammering at

one of the doors. 'Please come. Help! I need someone.'

But no one came and she had to go on running. There was a big glow coming from a building further along. She couldn't see it properly, of course, but her nose caught the thick grown-up smell of beer. It was a pub – and pubs were open when it was dark.

She ran until she got to the pub wall. She felt her way along the pebbledash surface until she got to the big space of the doorway. There was a huge lamp overhead. The light made her screw up her eyes and blink. She rubbed at them to try to get them to settle down and stepped right into the saloon bar.

There was a great buzz of conversation and a warm thick smoky smell and lights dazzling her in all directions.

'Here, what's up, little girl? You crying?

Been waiting for your daddy, have you?' said someone, pulling at her T-shirt.

'Please,' said Mary. She struggled to find the right words.

'Sorry, lovie, but there's no kiddies allowed in here. Out you go, there's a good girl.'

'Shame, leaving a little kid like that hanging around outside a pub!'

'Who's with this little girl, eh?'

'No! Don't find them! Don't let them get me!' Mary begged.

'No one's going to get you, dearie,' said a soft lady's voice. She squatted down until Mary could see a smiling face.

'Want to tell me all about it? Let's go into my sitting-room at the back where we'll be more cosy.'

She led Mary through to the back of the bar.

'There now. We'll soon sort you out,'

said the lady, settling her on a big sofa.

'You won't let the men in?' Mary repeated anxiously.

'Which men, dearie? I promise, no one's going to hurt you, not while I'm here. This is my pub and I say who can come in and who can't. You look as if you've been in the wars, poppet. What's the matter with your poor old eyes?'

'I can't see very well,' said Mary.

'Oh good heavens, you're not the little blind girl? The one on the news, the one that was kidnapped? We'd better phone the police right away.'

She dialled the number and spoke excitedly.

'Yes, I'm sure. She's sitting right here beside me. She's a bit grubby and she's got one or two bumps and bruises, but apart from that she seems OK. You are OK, aren't you, sweetheart?' she said to Mary.

'I-I think so,' said Mary.

The lady was very kind and brought her a drink of lemonade and some chocolates. Mary sat and sipped and swallowed, still in a daze. She kept thinking about Micky and the man with the knife. The lady told her she was safe now but Mary didn't feel sure. What if the man with the knife came running in and grabbed her the way he'd done in the post office?

Then she heard hurrying footsteps and she jumped to her feet in fright, spilling the lemonade.

'It's all right, dear. It's the police,' said the lady, putting her arm around her.

The room seemed suddenly full of big men and Mary couldn't help cowering away.

'Hello, Mary,' said a voice right up close. 'Yes, it is you. Your mummy's shown me a photo of you.'

'Is Mum very cross?' Mary whispered.

'She'll be overjoyed to know you're safe. We've sent a car straight round to fetch your mum and dad. They'll be here any minute now, pet. But while we're waiting for them, I wonder if you can be a really clever girl and tell me a bit about these nasty men who took you away. When did they let you go?'

'They didn't let me go. I escaped. I had to run and run,' said Mary. 'And they came after me.'

'Quick, lads, we'll do a search in the surrounding streets. Can you tell me anything at all about them, Mary?'

'Well. They're horrible,' said Mary.

'Yes, of course they are. And we're going to catch them and put them away in prison so they can't frighten anyone else. But we need to have some idea what they're like, so we know who to look for. I know you can't see much, Mary, but maybe you heard them talking. Did they have rough voices? Did they sound young or old?'

'One's older than the other. The one with the knife. Bob. And there's Micky, he's younger and he was a bit kind to me. He's fat. He bumped into me when he took me to the bathroom. And the knife man has got dirty trainers and jeans, and I think he's quite tall like my dad because he lifted me up, and he's ever so strong. He's got a horrible knife and a picture on his arm of a skull and some bones. There was a snake and big monkey too.'

'You little wonder! That's a much better description than most people could give!' said the policeman delightedly, dispatching some of his men. 'Now, Mary, where did this Bob and Micky take you?'

'It was Micky's flat. We went in the car and I tried to work out where we were going but we kept turning right and left and I can't remember all the roads though I did try.'

'Of course you can't. Now this flat – did you go up in a lift?'

'No, we went down. Down these steps. It smelt all old and mouldy.'

'A basement flat!'

'There's a car at the back, Bob told Micky to put a tarpaulin over it. It's quite near here, in a little street. When I got to the end of it I ran round into this big street with the shops and the pub. The railings at the top of the steps are all peeling and there's a dustbin down below, it's probably all tipped up now, because the man with the knife fell over it when he was chasing me. I got out of the bathroom. I climbed out of the window,' said Mary proudly.

'You're the cleverest little girl I've ever met,' said the policeman.

They all clustered round her, asking her more questions, telling her how bright and intelligent and grown up she was. Mary sat up straight and started smiling.

Then she heard someone calling.

'Mary! Mary! Oh, where is she?'

'Mum!' said Mary, standing up.

And then she was lifted up in the air and Mum was holding her and Dad had his arms around both of them, and Gran was there too, saying her name over and over again.

'Oh, Mary, I can't believe you're really safe,' said Mum, kissing and hugging her. 'We've been out of our minds with worry!'

'It's all my fault for falling asleep,' Gran wailed.

'Don't be silly, Gran. Now, Mary lovie, tell us what happened,' said Dad.

Mary opened her mouth to tell them but started to cry instead. She was furious. She wanted to tell them how clever she'd been and how she'd hardly cried all the time she was with the man with the knife, but now she was crying like a little baby.

'I'm . . . *not* . . . a . . . baby!' she sobbed.

'I'll say you're not,' said the senior policeman. 'Wait till you hear the wonderful description she's given us of these two villains. We'll get them, don't worry.'

They caught Micky almost straight away, still blundering around his flat. He kept blabbing that it wasn't his fault or his idea, it was all down to Bob – and he told the police Bob's address. They'd arrested him too before the night was over.

It was all over at long last for Mary too. Mum and Dad and Gran took her home and she had a hot bath and a special supper and was then carefully tucked up in her own bed. Gran was put to bed too, worn out with the worry and excitement. Mum and Dad came to sit with Mary while she went to sleep.

'Poor Gran,' said Mary guiltily. 'It was my fault, not hers.'

'Whatever made you go out by yourself like that, darling?' Mum asked.

'I wanted to show I wasn't a baby,' said Mary.

'Well, we know you're not a baby now,' said Dad. 'You've been very naughty but you've also been a big brave girl and we're very proud of you. We're not going to treat you like a baby any more, I promise.'

'But you're still not allowed to go to the shop by yourself,' said Mum, giving her another kiss.

'Not until you're older,' said Dad.

'I've done it. I don't want to any more,' said Mary, and she went to sleep, safe at last.